Cam Jansen

and the Summer Camp

Mysteries

A SUPER SPECIAL

Cam Jansen

and the Summer Camp
Mysteries

A SUPER SPECIAL

David A. Adler

illustrated by
Joy Allen

SCHOLASTIC INC.
New York   Toronto   London   Auckland   Sydney
Mexico City   New Delhi   Hong Kong   Buenos Aires

ISBN-13: 978-0-545-07786-6
ISBN-10: 0-545-07786-9

12 11 10 9 8 7 6 5 4 3   8 9 10 11 12 13/0

Printed in the U.S.A.   40

First Scholastic printing, January 2008

Set in New Baskerville

For Joseph C. Yellin, MD
—D.A.

CONTENTS

CamJansen

The First Day of Camp Mystery

CHAPTER ONE

"I was always busy at camp," Cam Jansen's mother said. "We played baseball. We swam. We played tennis. And at night, I shared my cabin with all my friends. It was a sleepover party that didn't end."

"But Danny is in my bunk," Cam's friend Eric Shelton said. "I'm sure he'll ask me riddles and tell me jokes all night. I'll never get to sleep."

Mrs. Jansen was driving Cam and Eric to Camp Eagle Lake. The children would be there for three weeks. Eric's father was in the car, too.

"Danny never stops!" Eric said, and shook his head. "How do you catch a squirrel? What's green and jumps?"

"The second one is easy," Eric's father said. "A frog is green and jumps."

"Well, that's not what Danny thinks. His answer is 'celery with hiccups.' And he says to catch a squirrel, 'you climb a tree and act like a nut.'"

Mrs. Jansen pointed to a sign on the side of the road. "Is this where we get off?" she asked. "It's exit fifty-four, but it doesn't say Camp Eagle Lake. Oh, I wish I had brought the directions."

"Did you drive sixty-three miles?" Mr. Shelton asked. "I remember something in the directions about sixty-three miles."

"I looked at the directions this morning," Cam said.

She closed her eyes and said, *"Click."*

Cam says *"click"* when she wants to remember something. She has what people call a photographic memory. It's as if she has a mental camera that takes pictures of

4

whatever she sees. Cam says that *"click"* is the sound her camera makes.

"When you get off the bridge, take the State Highway for fifty-four miles to exit sixty-three," Cam said with her eyes closed. "Follow Millard Fillmore Road to the camp entrance."

Eric blinked his eyes. *"Click! Click!"* he said. "Cam's camera will get us there!"

When Cam was younger, people called her Jennifer, her real name. But when they found out about her amazing memory, they called her "The Camera." Soon "The Camera" became just "Cam."

"Look at all the cows and horses," Mrs. Jansen said as she drove. "Camp Eagle Lake is in the middle of farm country."

Cam opened her eyes.

Cam, Eric, and Mr. Shelton looked out their windows. They saw lots of animals, farms, and billboards. At exit sixty-three there was a sign for Camp Eagle Lake.

Mrs. Jansen smiled and said, "Cam, you were right."

She turned at the exit and followed the signs to the camp.

There was a line of cars waiting to get in.

"You know, we can't stay long," Mrs. Jansen told Cam and Eric while they waited.

"The camp director sent us a schedule," Mr. Shelton added. "Your groups will meet on the baseball field. We'll go there with you. Then we'll go with you to your bunks to help you unpack. You'll get ready for lunch and we'll go home."

One by one the cars stopped at the entrance, the drivers spoke to someone sitting in a booth, and the cars entered the camp. Soon it was Mrs. Jansen's turn. She lowered her window.

Mrs. Jansen told the old man in the booth, "Our children Jennifer Jansen and Eric Shelton are campers here."

The man wore a HELLO MY NAME IS BARRY sticker on his shirt.

"They should have name tags like mine," he said. "Please, have them put on their tags."

Cam and Eric put on their tags. Barry checked their names on a list. Then he smiled and said, "Jennifer and Eric, welcome to Camp Eagle Lake. You're the last campers to arrive."

Barry told Mrs. Jansen to park in the visitors' parking area along the side of the road. "After you've parked," he said, "walk down the road to the large baseball field in the center of camp. The children are gathering there."

Mrs. Jansen found a tight spot by a big tree near the very front of the visitors' lot. Mr. Shelton got out of the car first. He walked ahead to look for the baseball field.

Mrs. Jansen stood by her car. "Look at all the trees. It's so green and quiet here," she said, and took a deep breath. "The air is so fresh."

Cam smiled.

"There are lots of fields and tennis courts," Mr. Shelton said when he came back. "This road goes right through the

center of the camp. We just have to walk along it to get to the baseball field. And there's a locked box for Cam's and Eric's spending and snack money. They won't have to worry about losing it."

He led them down the road to a large blue metal box. Taped to the top of it was a sign: PLACE SNACK MONEY HERE. Beneath that, in smaller print, were instructions: *Put money in an envelope. Write your child's name and bunk number on the front. Seal the envelope and deposit it here.*

Next to the box was a stack of envelopes.

Cam and Eric followed the instructions. They put their envelopes through the flap in the front of the box. Then they all went back to the car. Mrs. Jansen opened the trunk. Mr. Shelton took out Eric's suitcase, hockey stick, tennis racket, baseball glove, baseball bat, and a bag of books to read during rest hour. Cam just brought a suitcase, tennis racket, and books. She took her things out of the trunk.

"Let me help," Mrs. Jansen said.

Cam gave her mother the tennis racket.

"Give me something," Mr. Shelton said to Eric. "I'll help you."

"No, thank you," Eric said. "You have my suitcase. I can carry this stuff."

Eric had his baseball glove on his left hand. His hockey stick was pointed straight up. His baseball bat was under his right arm. His tennis racket was under his left arm. He held his book bag in his right hand. It was dragging on the ground.

"Let's go," Eric said.

He rushed ahead and his tennis racket fell. He bent to pick it up and dropped his baseball bat. He picked up the bat and his hockey stick fell.

Eric reached the road and stopped. He put down his bag of books.

"I've got to rest," he said.

Honk! Honk!

Someone in a car was just leaving the parking lot and wanted to get past. Eric picked up the book bag. He bent down to get the hockey stick and dropped his baseball glove.

Mr. Shelton took out a digital camera. "What a great picture," he said, and pressed the shutter. "Got it," he said.

Cam was standing next to Mr. Shelton. *"Click!"* she said, and blinked her eyes. "I have the picture, too."

Honk!

Mr. Shelton hurried to Eric. He took the

book bag. Eric and his father stepped to the side and the car drove past. As they continued down the road, Cam saw lots of children and their parents on the baseball field. There were lots of signs, too.

"There's Danny," Cam said. "He's standing in the outfield, by the B8 sign."

"I'm in B8," Eric said. "That's my group. The 'B' is for boys."

"There's my group, G8," Cam said. "It's meeting right next to B8. Let's go. I want to meet the other girls in my bunk."

CHAPTER TWO

The groups of younger children, six- and seven-year-olds, were in the infield. Cam hurried past them to the people gathered around the G8 sign. A tall teenage girl with long brown hair held out her hand. HELLO. MY NAME IS FRAN, COUNSELOR G8 was written on her name tag.

Cam shook her hand.

Fran looked at Cam's tag. "Welcome to camp, Jennifer."

"Most people call me Cam."

Fran smiled. She held her hands to her heart, looked up, fluttered her eyes, and joked, "Most people call me 'Beautiful.'"

Fran laughed.

She introduced Cam to the girls in her group.

"Now we're all here," a girl named Terri told Cam. "There are eight girls in G8. That's about average for this camp. This is my third summer at Eagle Lake. Three weeks here is just five hundred and four hours. I wish it was more."

"Save me! Save me!" Eric called out as he ran to Cam. "Danny won't stop asking me riddles."

"I'll stop. I'll stop," Danny shouted as he followed Eric.

Cam introduced Eric and Danny to Terri.

"We're in B8," Eric said.

"We play your bunk in baseball," Terri said.

"Hey," Danny asked Terri. "Do you know why Cinderella was no good at baseball?"

Terri shook her head. She didn't know.

"She ran away from the ball," Danny said. "That's why."

Terri shook hear head again.

"Don't you get it?" Danny asked. "In the story, at midnight, she ran away from the prince's ball."

"You said you'd stop," Eric told Danny. "Now stop!"

"But I didn't tell *you* a joke. I told Terri. And she likes jokes."

"No," she said. "I like math."

"Oh," Danny said. "Do you like baseball, too? Can you hit?"

"I can hit a little," Terri said. Then she pointed to a girl sitting on the grass who was reading a book. "Do you see her? That's Gina. She's better at baseball than anyone. Last year she hit a ball into the trees."

Tall evergreens surrounded the field.

"Do you know what she did after she crossed home plate?" Terri asked. "She picked up her book and read some more. Gina loves books."

Cam's mother and Mr. Shelton joined them.

"You have to hear Danny's highway joke," Mr. Shelton told Cam's mother. "Go on, Danny. Tell her."

"I can't," Danny said. "I promised not to tell any more jokes."

"Okay, I'll tell it," Mr. Shelton said. "Why did the orange stop on the highway?"

Mrs. Jansen shrugged. She didn't know.

"It ran out of juice."

Mrs. Jansen didn't laugh. She just said, "That's very nice."

"Good morning," a voice called out. *"Welcome to Camp Eagle Lake. I'm Sadie Rosen, the camp director."*

Sadie Rosen was talking through the camp loudspeakers.

"Counselors, please take your campers to their bunks. Parents, you may help your children with their things. Then say good-bye, and have a safe trip home."

A teenage boy walked over. HELLO. MY NAME IS JACOB, COUNSELOR B8 was written on his tag.

"Eric and Danny," he said. "You can't just wander off. Let's go. We're all going to the bunk now."

"Yes, Eric. You must listen to your counselor," Mr. Shelton told his son. Then he turned to Mrs. Jansen and said, "This camp is so well organized. The schedule. The name tags. The lock box."

"Lock box," Jacob asked. "What lock box?"

"The box by the parking lot. It's blue and looks like a mailbox," Mr. Shelton told him. "We put Eric's and Cam's spending money in there."

"This is my first year here," Jacob said. "I don't know about a lock box."

Jacob called Fran over. She had a camp handbook. She gave it to Jacob and he opened it. "Look! It says right here, 'Campers should give their snack money to their counselors for safekeeping. It is the counselors' responsibility to keep a strict accounting of all camper funds in their care.' There's nothing here about a blue mailbox."

"Well, it's a good idea," Mr. Shelton said. "Things could get lost at camp."

Jacob said, "I'd like to see that box. And I'd like to know why Sadie Rosen didn't tell us about it."

"Come on," Eric said. "I'll show it to you."

Terri said, "My dad put my money in that box and my younger brother's money, too."

"Not everyone in my group saw it," Fran said. "Some of them gave me their snack money."

She gave Jacob a few envelopes and asked him to put them in the box. She told Jacob she would watch B8.

Terri's dad was with her younger brother. She told her dad she was going with Cam, Eric, their parents, and Jacob to the lock box.

"There are thirty bunks," Terri said as they walked across the baseball field. "With eight kids in each bunk, that's two hundred forty envelopes, and thousands of dollars."

Jacob stopped near home plate. He asked Matthew, the counselor of B1, the youngest boys' group, if he knew about the box.

"Yes, the kids told me, and I think it's great," Matthew said. "I don't like being responsible for other people's money."

He gave Jacob the envelopes he had collected and asked him to put them in the box.

"But there's nothing about it in the handbook," Jacob said.

"It's the same handbook we had last year," Matthew told him. "Sadie Rosen probably didn't put in the new stuff."

They reached the road that went through the center of camp.

"It's over there," Eric said, "right under that tree at the edge of the visitors' parking lot."

Eric led Jacob and the others to the tree, but the lock box was gone.

Chapter Three

"Maybe the box is under another tree," Jacob said. "Maybe it's at the other end of the parking lot."

"No," Eric told him. "I'm sure it was right here."

"There's my car," Mrs. Jansen said, and pointed. "The box was just down the road from it."

"Maybe it's on the other side of the road," Jacob said. "Let's look."

Eric, Terri, and Mr. Shelton walked with Jacob through the parking lot. Cam and Mrs. Jansen didn't. Cam stood by her mother's car, closed her eyes, and said, *"Click!"*

"There was a red car next to ours," Cam said with her eyes still closed, "and then three more cars."

"They're all still here," her mother said.

"Just beyond the blue car," Cam said, "is a maple tree with a funny crooked branch. That's where we saw the box."

Cam opened her eyes. She walked to the tree and said, "It was right here. And look, you can even see marks in the dirt. That proves we're right."

Cam and Mrs. Jansen waited by the tree. When Eric and the others returned, Cam showed them the marks.

"I bet I know what happened," Jacob said. "The box was here, just where you said. Then Sadie Rosen took it into the camp office."

Cam noticed Danny waving to them from near the baseball field. He ran to them.

He told Jacob, "The Sadie woman wants

to know where you are. She wants you to take our group from the baseball field to the bunk."

"And I want to know," Jacob said, "what to do with all these envelopes."

Jacob walked quickly back to the baseball field. It was hard to keep up with him.

"Hey," Danny called. "Wait up. I want to ask you something."

Jacob stopped and waited. When Danny caught up, he asked, "What did the balloon say to the pin?"

"That's your question?" Jacob shouted. "Are you going to ask me silly riddles for the next three weeks?"

"It's okay if you don't know the answer," Danny said. "You don't have to get angry."

Jacob started walking again. He walked even faster now. Danny ran beside him.

"The balloon said, 'Hello, Buster,'" Danny told him.

Jacob pretended not to hear Danny. He just kept walking. When he reached the edge of the baseball field, he waved to a woman standing by second base. In one hand, the woman held a clipboard and lots of papers. She waved back, and Jacob walked across the field to her.

"Where were you?" the woman asked. "It's time to take your children to the bunk."

The woman had short gray hair. She was dressed in a blue sweat suit and around her neck was a whistle on a chain. Her tag said, HELLO. MY NAME IS SADIE ROSEN, CAMP DIRECTOR.

Jacob showed her his handful of envelopes. "I have all these," he said, "but I can't find the lock box."

"What box?" Sadie Rosen asked.

Cam, Eric, Terri, and their parents had caught up with Jacob.

"The blue metal box by the parking lot," Mr. Shelton said. "It was for the snack money. There was a sign on it telling us what to do."

Cam closed her eyes and said, *"Click!"*

"The sign said, *'Put money in an envelope,'*

Cam said with her eyes still closed. "'*Write your child's name and bunk number on the front. Seal the envelope and deposit it here.*'"

"There's no box for snack money," Sadie Rosen said.

Cam opened her eyes.

Mrs. Jansen told her, "Well, there was a box, and lots of people put money in it."

"If only half the campers did," Terri said, "there would be thousands of dollars in there."

"If you don't know anything about the box," Mr. Shelton said, "then someone must have put it by the parking lot to steal the money." He shook his head and said, "It's all gone now."

CHAPTER FOUR

"No one stole your money," Sadie Rosen said. "This must be a prank. Someone thinks this is funny."

She looked at Jacob.

"I don't think it's funny," he said. "I didn't know anything about the box until these campers told me."

Sadie Rosen asked Cam and Terri, "Who's your counselor?"

"Fran."

"She couldn't have taken it," Jacob said. "She's been with her children the whole time. Right now she's watching mine, too."

Sadie Rosen looked around. Most of the counselors were leading their campers to their bunks.

Tweet! Tweet!

Sadie Rosen blew her whistle and everyone stopped. She walked to Matthew, the B1 counselor, and asked him if he knew about the blue box. Lots of children and their parents were nearby.

"Yes," Matthew said. "Jacob told me about it. Then I asked my campers. Most of them said they had already put their money in it."

"It's not a camp box," Ms. Rosen said. "I don't know who put it there."

"What about our money?" one of the parents asked.

"I don't know," Sadie Rosen told her.

"You don't know?" the woman said. "Does that mean our money was stolen?"

The woman turned and said really loudly, "Did you hear that! Our children's snack money was stolen!"

The bad news spread from one group to the next. Lots more parents and their children gathered around Sadie Rosen.

"What about our money?" they asked.

"Who stole it?"

"I blame the camp."

"Where's my money," one little boy cried. "I want my snack money!"

Tweet! Tweet!

Sadie Rosen blew her whistle and everyone was quiet.

"Someone put a blue box by the parking lot," she said. "Some of you may have put your children's snack money in there."

"I did!" someone called out.

"So did I," many others shouted.

"Well," Sadie Rosen said, "we don't know who put the box there or who took it away."

Children and their parents started talking again. Some were angry. Ms. Rosen held up her hands.

"I promise you," she said, "we will do everything we can to get your money back."

"And what if you don't?" someone asked.

"I assure you, every child will get snacks," Sadie Rosen said. "Now please, go to your bunks. Unpack. At noon we'll have lunch."

Most of the children, their counselors, and their parents walked toward the bunks. Cam, Eric, Terri, Danny, and their parents didn't.

Ms. Rosen took a cell phone from her pocket. She pushed a few buttons.

"Let's go," Jacob told Eric and Danny.

"I want to stay here with Cam," Eric said. "We're good at solving mysteries."

Eric told Jacob and the others about Cam's amazing memory. "We have solved lots of mysteries together. Once we even found a thief who stole diamonds from a jewelry store."

Ms. Rosen held her cell phone by her ear. "This is Camp Eagle Lake. I need to report a robbery," she said. "Please, send some police officers."

"Let's go," Jacob told Danny.

"I'll go with you," Danny told him. "I have some more questions to ask you."

"Please, no more riddles," Jacob said. "And Terri, you should come with me, too. I'll take you to G8."

Danny, Terri, and their parents went with Jacob.

Sadie Rosen put the cell phone in her pocket. Then she noticed that Cam, Eric, and their parents were standing beside her.

"You should be with your groups," she told Cam and Eric.

"But we want to solve the mystery," Eric said. "We want to find the blue lock box."

"The police will handle this," Sadie Rosen told them. "It's time to go to your bunks and unpack."

They picked up their things and walked off the baseball field and onto the road. Beyond the road were the tennis courts.

"Wait!" Eric said. He saw something and pointed to the courts. "I think I've done it. I think I found the thief."

CHAPTER FIVE

Eric gave his father and Mrs. Jansen all the things he was carrying. Then he ran across the road to the tennis courts. A man there was pulling a large trunk on wheels.

Eric stopped in front of the man and held up his hands.

"You thought you could get away!" Eric told him. "Well, I caught you."

The man smiled and said, "Yes. I did get away. I got away for the whole summer. I live in the city, and it's very hot there right now."

"And I know what's in that trunk," Eric

said. "There's a lock box in there. It's filled with everything you stole."

"The only thing I ever stole," the man said, "is second base. Watch out for me when I play baseball. I'm a great base runner."

"That trunk and that box are filled with money," Eric said.

"Money!" the man said, and looked at the trunk. "I hope you're right."

Cam and the others caught up with Eric.

"Eric," Mr. Shelton told his son. "He's not a thief. Look at his name tag."

HELLO. MY NAME IS JIM, SPORTS DIRECTOR was written on his tag.

Jim put down the trunk. He took a key from his pocket and opened it. Baseballs, basketballs, and tennis balls fell out. They rolled across the tennis court.

Tweet! Tweet!

Sadie Rosen had blown her whistle. She was walking toward them.

"Why aren't you in your bunks?" she asked the children. "And why is all this stuff on the tennis courts?"

"It's my fault," Eric said. "I thought he had the lock box in there."

"We'll take them to their bunks," Mr. Shelton said, "but first I want to help Eric pick up all this stuff."

"I'll help, too," Cam said.

Eric ran after a basketball that had rolled across the road. Cam ran after some tennis balls.

"Wait," Mrs. Jansen called to them. "Be

careful. Look both ways. A car might be coming."

"Why would a car be coming in? All the kids and their parents are already here," Eric said.

Cam stopped. "That's right," she said. "And no parent would be leaving now, not before helping his or her child unpack."

Eric crossed the road. He picked up the basketball.

Cam folded her arms.

"I should have thought of that," she said. Cam stood still at the edge of the road. She closed her eyes and said, *"Click!"*

Eric stopped. He saw that Cam's eyes were closed.

"Did you *click?*" he asked. "Did you remember something?"

"Yes," Cam answered. Her eyes were still closed. "I may know who took the box."

Just then a blue-and-white car entered the camp. It stopped by the camp entrance.

"Look," Eric said. "The police are here."

Cam opened her eyes. The police car stopped at the camp entrance for just a moment. Then it drove slowly past the baseball field and around the tennis courts.

"I have to talk to the police," Cam said. "I have to tell them what I just remembered."

CHAPTER SIX

The police car rode past Cam and Eric to the other side of the tennis courts. Cam ran after it. Eric dropped the basketball he had in his hands and followed her.

The police car stopped by the edge of the tennis court, right where Sadie Rosen, Cam's mother, and Eric's father were waiting.

Two police officers got out. They were talking to Ms. Rosen. A tall officer with bright red hair and a red mustache was taking notes on a small pad.

As Cam and Eric reached their parents and Sadie Rosen, they heard Ms. Rosen say, "I never saw the thief. I never even saw the box."

"But I did," Eric said. "I saw the box. It's large and blue and has a flap in the front just like a mailbox."

"And I saw the thief," Cam said.

"No you didn't," Eric told her. "I was with you all morning and we didn't see any thief."

"Maybe you didn't, but *I* did," Cam said. Cam closed her eyes and said, *"Click!"*

"I'm looking at him right now," Cam said with her eyes still closed. "I know he has dark hair and was wearing sunglasses. But that's all I know. I didn't see him too well."

"What are you talking about? Why are your eyes closed?" Sadie Rosen asked.

Mrs. Jansen told her about Cam's amazing memory.

"A car honked at us when we were walking to the baseball field this morning. Someone was leaving camp. But why was he leaving camp when everyone else was just coming in?" Cam asked.

"Hey," Mr. Shelton said. "I remember that car. I think I have a picture of it on my digital camera."

Mr. Shelton took out his camera. He found the picture he had taken of Eric with his hockey stick, tennis racket, and other things.

"Look here," he said. "That's the car that was leaving camp. It's blue."

The two police officers looked at the picture. The red-haired officer took out his pad. He flipped it open and wrote *blue car, male, sunglasses,* and *dark hair* on the first clean page.

The other officer looked at the pad and said, "A man with dark hair and sunglasses, driving a blue car, was leaving camp before everyone else. That's not much."

"But this clicking girl is right," Sadie Rosen said. "Parents never leave camp early. On the first day, I always have trouble getting them to go home. They want to talk to their children. Watch their children. See what's for lunch."

"She may be right about the man and the car," the officer said. "But we can't stop every blue car we find."

"Wait," Cam said. "Maybe I can tell you more."

Cam closed her eyes again. She said, *"Click!"*

"I can see the car," she said. "I can see the license plate."

Cam told the officer the license plate number.

The red-haired officer wrote down the number. He closed his pad and said, "Now we have enough clues. We'll look for the car. We'll let you know if we find the box and the money."

"And Barry, the man at the gate, may be able to describe the man," Sadie Rosen said. "He sees everyone who comes in here."

The officers got into their car. Cam and the others followed them to the entrance.

Barry said, "When that man came in, he didn't give me his name. He pointed to the car just ahead and said, 'I'm with them.' When he left, he drove past me really fast."

The red-haired officer wrote some notes

on his pad. Then he said, "We'll go looking for him."

Sadie Rosen thanked the officers. Then she told Cam and Eric, "Now, please go to your bunks."

"Can't we wait?" Eric asked. "We want to know if the police catch him."

"No, I'm sorry. You can't," Sadie Rosen said. "It's time for you to unpack. And I'm sure your parents want to get on the road before the late afternoon traffic."

Mr. Shelton nodded. "It sounds like the police have everything under control."

"Let's go," Mrs. Jansen said to Cam and Eric.

CHAPTER SEVEN

Cam's bunk was on the girls' campus, to the right of the dining hall. Eric's was on the boys' campus, to the left.

In the middle of a row of small bunk buildings was one with a large sign that said G8. Cam and her mother went into the bunk.

There was a row of cots on each side of the large room. Beside each bed was a wooden nightstand. Girls and their parents were making beds and putting things in the nightstands. At the other end of the bunk was a place to hang clothing. Beyond that were sinks, showers, and bathrooms.

Cam found the only empty bed. Her mother helped her unpack.

"It's almost noon," Fran announced. "It's time to say good-bye to your parents."

"Here," Mrs. Jansen whispered. She gave Cam some money. "If they don't find the thief and the box, you'll have this for snacks."

"But Mom..."

"Just take it," Mrs. Jansen said. "And if they catch the thief, you'll have extra snack money."

Mrs. Jansen hugged Cam.

"I'll miss you," Mrs. Jansen said. There were tears in her eyes.

"I'll miss you, too, Mom. But I'll be fine. I'm already having a good time. Trying to solve that snack money mystery was fun."

Mrs. Jansen and the other parents left the bunk.

At lunch, Cam sat next to Terri, the math whiz. Terri told Cam all about camp.

"We swim in a lake," Terri said. "It's better than a pool, because it's bigger. But after it rains, the water is cold. And arts and crafts is great. Last year I made a jewelry box."

After lunch, the G8 girls stood by their table in the dining room. Fran stood with them and held up a Camp Eagle Lake sign. "Smile!" Jim, the sports counselor, said, and took their picture.

The G8 girls went back to their bunk. They changed clothes and got ready for tennis. They were walking to the courts when

Cam's and Eric's names were announced on the camp loudspeakers.

Jennifer Jansen and Eric Shelton, please report to the main office.

"It's right by the main entrance," Terri said.

Cam walked across the tennis courts to the office. A police car was parked outside. The two police officers and Sadie Rosen were inside. Eric was there, too. He was wearing a bathing suit.

He told Cam, "We were on our way to the lake."

"We found the thief," the red-haired officer told Cam and Eric. "The blue box was in the backseat of his car."

"Thanks to both of you," Sadie Rosen said, "we have all the snack money."

Sadie Rosen smiled.

"Aren't you going to give these children a reward?" the red-haired officer asked.

"A reward?" Ms. Rosen said.

She thought for a moment.

"Yes. Tomorrow everyone in bunks B8

and G8 will get ice-cream sundaes."

When they left the office, Cam told Eric about the extra snack money her mother had given her.

Eric said, "My dad gave me extra money, too. He thought the police might not catch the thief. But I told him, of course they will. They have my friend Cam helping them."

CamJansen

It's a *RAID!*

CHAPTER ONE

Cam had made lots of new friends at camp. She played number games with Terri and told her about the many mysteries she and Eric had solved.

Cam and Gina traded books.

Betsy's family liked to travel. She told Cam about the faraway places she had visited.

One afternoon, during the second week of camp, Cam and the girls of G8 were getting out of the lake when Fran came to take them back to their bunk. Kitty, the camp's pet cat, was following her.

"I'm sorry I'm late," Fran told the swim

counselor. "Jacob and I were in the middle of a great game of tennis. I won."

Fran walked to the edge of the lake. She put both hands in the water. "Nice and warm," she said. "So how did my G8 ducks enjoy their swim lessons?"

"They did very well," the swim counselor told her.

Kitty looked up at Betsy.

Meow!

Fran called out to the girls, "We're going back to the bunk to get changed. Baseball is next."

Cam and the other girls in G8 wrapped themselves in their towels. They walked quickly ahead, up the small hill near the lake to their bunk. Fran and Kitty followed them.

"Hey, Cam," Terri called as they walked. "Do you know how many times this summer we'll take this walk from the lake?"

Cam shook her head. She didn't know.

"Oh, that's easy," Terri said. "We go to the lake every day for swimming and three

times a week for canoeing. Over three weeks, that's thirty times."

They were walking across the small, grassy field near their bunk.

"Hurry and change into shorts, T-shirts, and sneakers," Fran told them. "And remember to get your baseball gloves."

Cam was the first one to step into the bunk.

Cam quickly looked around the room,

then she shouted, "Hey, what happened?"

Beds had been pushed into the middle of the bunk. Sneakers and pants were piled on the beds. Shirts were hanging from the rafters. *Hello G8! Guess Who!* was written in chalk on the ceiling.

The other G8 girls hurried into the bunk. "Who did this?" Terri asked.

"I didn't," Betsy said. "I was at the lake." Just then Fran and Kitty entered the bunk. "It's a raid!" Fran shouted. "It's a raid!" Fran clapped her hands and sang,

> *"Don't be afraid.*
> *It's just a raid.*
> *We'll get even.*
> *Even-Steven.*
> *Raid! Raid! Raid!"*

The G8 girls laughed and clapped along.

"But who should we get even-Steven with?" Terri asked. "Who did this?"

"I think it was G9," Betsy said. "They are always racing us to the dining room and saying they're better than us. Or maybe B8. We play them in baseball."

"Whoever did this didn't steal my money," Terri said. "I had eight dimes, three nickels, and twelve pennies in the cup by my bed and it's all still here."

Gina found her bed and started to push it back to its spot.

"We'll clean up later," Fran told her. "Right now we have to get ready for baseball. While you're playing, I'll be thinking." She pointed to her head and grinned. "Thinking of ways to get even."

Cam and the other girls searched on the beds for their sneakers. There was a large lump beneath the blanket of one of the beds. Terri lifted the blanket and found their baseball gloves.

Fran stood by the door to the bunk.

"You know what we'll do?" Fran said. "We'll figure out who raided our bunk and we'll move all their beds onto the grass. We'll fill their left sneakers with popcorn

and hide all their right sneakers. They'll have to hop."

Betsy said, "No. We'll put potato chips in their sneakers. It will be so funny hearing them crunch as they walk."

"Popcorn and potato chips," Fran laughed. "This is so exciting."

"But first we have to know who raided us," Terri said. "It's a mystery, and Cam has solved lots of those. Maybe she'll solve this one, too."

CHAPTER TWO

"I solve mysteries by remembering something I've seen," Cam told Terri as they walked to the baseball field. "But I don't think I've seen anything that could help. When we left for the lake, our bunk was neat. When we came back, it was a mess. That's all I know. I don't know if that's enough to figure out who raided us."

"Close your eyes and say, *'Click!'* Terri suggested. "That should help."

"Not now," Cam said. "I can't close my eyes while I'm walking."

"Yes you can. I'll hold your hand. You won't get lost or bump into anything."

Terri took Cam's hand. Then Cam closed her eyes and said, *"Click!"*

"I'm looking at the bunk now," Cam said with her eyes closed. "I'm looking at how it was just before we went to the lake. The beds were all against the wall. The bunk was very neat."

Terri led Cam onto the baseball field.

"Click!" Cam said again.

"Now I'm looking at the bunk when we came back from the lake. It was a real mess. There was even writing on the ceiling."

"Sit down," Terri told Cam. "There's a bench behind you."

Cam opened her eyes. She looked back. Then she sat on the bench.

"I didn't see any clues," Cam said. "I just saw a neat bunk and a messy bunk."

Eric and Danny's group, B8, was already on the field. Cam's team was hitting first.

Fran told each girl when she would bat. Cam would bat fifth, right after Terri. Fran also told each girl which position she would play in the field. Cam would play third base.

Cam sat on the bench next to Terri. They waited for their turns to bat.

Betsy was up first. Jim, the sports director, was pitching for both teams. He was the umpire, too.

Betsy hit the ball toward Eric at shortstop. He moved over a few steps and caught it.

"Maybe Eric knows something about the raid," Terri said. "Betsy thought it might be B8. Let's ask Eric."

Cam and Terri walked along the left side of the field.

"Eric!" Cam called. "I need to ask you something."

"We're in the middle of a game," Jim told Cam and Terri. "Ask him later."

Cam and Terri sat on the ground by third base, right beside where Danny was playing.

"Ask me," Danny whispered.

Terri asked, "Did you raid our bunk?"

"Maybe."

"Don't talk to Danny," Cam said. "Everything is a joke to him."

Stacy swung and missed three times. She struck out.

Gina was up next. She hit the ball high over the center fielder's head. She ran around the bases for a home run. The girls of G8 cheered. Gina smiled. Then she went to her seat on the bench and picked up her book.

"Terri," Fran called. "You're up."

Terri hurried to the backstop. She took a bat and stood by home plate.

"So, what happened to your bunk?" Danny

asked Cam. "Were there jokes written on the walls? Pajamas hanging from the ceiling? Jelly on the doorknob?"

"No," Cam told him. "No jokes and no jelly, so now I know you didn't do it."

Terri swung. She hit the ball toward third base.

"It's yours, Danny," Eric shouted.

Danny turned just as the ball bounced in front of him. The ball rolled past him and he ran after it. While Danny chased the ball, Terri ran to second base.

Now it was Cam's turn at bat.

She held her bat up and looked out at Jim. But suddenly she had an idea.

"That might be it!" Cam said.

Cam closed her eyes and said, *"Click!"*

Jim threw the ball.

"Strike one," Jim called. "That ball was right over the plate."

"Hey! Open your eyes," Fran shouted. "Baseball is more fun that way."

"Click!" Cam said again.

Jim threw the ball.

"Strike two," Jim called.

"I've got it," Cam said and opened her eyes just as Jim threw the ball the third time.

"Strike three," Jim said. "You're out."

"That's it," Cam said. "I know how to solve this mystery."

CHAPTER THREE

Terri ran in from second base. She took her glove from the bench. Then she asked Cam, "What happened?"

"I *clicked* and saw something. We know our bunk was raided while we were at the lake. But every group is busy. It could only have been a group that was playing near our bunk. I *clicked* and remembered that the basketball courts are right by our bunk."

Cam and Terri walked out onto the field. Cam stopped close to third base. Terri's position was shortstop, about twenty feet from Cam.

"We've got to find out," Cam said, "who was at the basketball courts while we were at the lake."

Jim turned to check if everyone was in position and ready to play.

"Jim would know," Cam said.

Cam and Terri ran to him.

"Who was playing basketball on the courts just before we got here?" they asked.

"I don't know. Now get back to your positions."

"But you have a schedule," Terri said.

Jim turned away from Terri. He was about to pitch. Cam ran back to third base. Terri ran back to shortstop.

Danny was the first to bat. He had his hat on backwards. He held his bat at the wrong end. He turned and faced Gina, the catcher, and said, "I'm ready."

Jim threw the ball over the middle of the plate.

"Strike one!"

"Hey," Danny said, and turned to face Jim. "I wasn't ready."

Danny turned his hat and bat around.

"Are you ready now?" Jim asked.

Danny nodded.

Jim pitched the ball. Danny hit it on the ground toward Terri, who fielded it and threw to first base.

As he ran, Danny waved his arms and yelled, "Ready or not, here I come."

The ball reached the base long before he did. Danny was out.

The next batter swung three times and missed.

There were two outs now as Eric came to the plate. He waved to Cam. Then he waited for Jim to pitch.

Eric hit the first pitch high into the air, but not very far. Cam stood under it, waited, and caught the ball for the third out. Cam took the ball back to Jim.

"Just a minute," Jim said. He picked up the clipboard that was on the ground by his feet. He looked at the top page.

"B8 was on two of the basketball courts. G9 was on the other two."

Cam stopped Eric on his way onto the field.

"Did your group raid our bunk?"

"No," Eric said. "I wouldn't do that."

"Did you see any of the girls from G9 leave the basketball courts?" Cam asked. "While you were playing basketball earlier, our bunk was raided. It was a real mess when we came back from the lake."

"I really don't know about G9," Eric said. "And I've got to get to my position."

Eric started toward his shortstop position. Then he stopped and called to Cam, "If you're solving a mystery, I want to help."

Cam sat on the bench next to Terri. "It wasn't Eric's bunk that raided us, so it must have been G9," Cam said. "They were playing near our bunk. It would have been easy for one or two of the girls to sneak off."

Cam and Terri watched three girls take their turns at bat. Each of them struck out.

On their way back into the field Terri said, "Wait till we get even with G9. Fran will help us plan lots of mischief."

"First I have to be sure," Cam said as she walked toward third base. "I don't want to put popcorn or potato chips in G9's sneakers if they didn't raid us."

It happened when we were at the lake, Cam thought while she stood in the field. *It had to be a group that was nearby.*

The first two batters hit the ball to the outfield. Laura caught them both.

But maybe it wasn't G9. Maybe another group did it, Cam thought. *The younger girls' groups pass our bunk all the time.*

The ball was hit on the ground.

"Get it! Get it!" Fran shouted.

Cam looked at Fran. Then she looked for the ball. It was headed right between her and Terri. Luckily Terri had been paying attention to the game. She ran to her right, reached down, and got the ball. She threw it to first base for the third out.

On her way back to the bench, Cam passed Eric.

"G9 didn't do it," Eric said. "I've been thinking about it and I'm sure. We were on the basketball courts closest to your bunk. If anyone from G9 raided your bunk, she would have walked past us. And no one did."

Maybe, Cam thought, *one of the younger girls' bunks did it.*

CHAPTER FOUR

When they sat on the bench Terri told Cam, "I don't want to put popcorn in anyone's sneakers. I just want whoever messed up our bunk to put everything back where it was. The beds. The sneakers. The shirts. The pants. Raids are just a big mess."

Cam nodded. She also didn't want to fill sneakers with popcorn. She'd rather *eat* popcorn and potato chips. And she wanted to solve this mystery.

G8 got a few hits and scored two runs. Then Terri grounded out. It was Cam's turn to bat.

"Let's go!" Fran shouted. "Hit it a mile!"

Cam stepped up to the plate. She looked out at Jim and waited. He pitched and Cam swung. She hit the ball just out of the reach of the first baseman. The ball rolled into the outfield.

Cam ran to first base.

"Go," Fran shouted. "Keep going!"

Cam kept running.

"Stop!" Fran shouted and held up her hands.

Cam stopped on second base.

"Nice hit," Eric said.

Laura, the next batter, stood at the plate. Jim pitched and Laura swung.

Cam started toward third base.

Laura hit the ball right at Eric near second base. He caught it and Laura was out. He raced to the base, stepped on it, and Cam was out, too.

"Nice going," Jim said. "It's a double play."

Tweet! Tweet! He blew his whistle.

"That's it," he called. "We'll finish the game tomorrow."

"We have tennis next," Eric told Cam as they walked off the field. "But first we have to go back to our bunk to get our rackets and tennis balls."

Cam stopped. "What did you just say?" she asked.

"We have tennis next," Eric said.

"Yes, and of course you need a tennis racket to play tennis." Cam smiled.

She folded her arms and thought for a moment.

"I think you did it," she told Eric. "I think you helped me solve another mystery."

Cam closed her eyes. She said, *"Click!"* She said, *"Click!"* again.

Cam opened her eyes and told Eric, "Come with me. I think I know who raided our bunk."

Eric followed Cam off the field. They walked toward Fran and Terri.

"Hi, Fran," Cam said, and smiled. "When you came to the lake you should have told us our bunk was such a mess."

"How would she know it was a mess?" Terri asked.

"Fran was playing tennis while we were swimming," Cam said. "But she didn't have her tennis racket with her when she came to the lake."

"That's right," Terri said. "If she put her racket away before she came to pick us up, she would have seen the mess."

"Fran, you dipped both of your hands in the lake and said, 'Nice and warm.'"

"It *was* nice and warm," Fran said.

"But I bet you didn't care how warm the water was," Cam said. "I bet you dipped your hands in the water to wash off the chalk dust."

"What chalk dust?" Fran asked.

"You used chalk to write HELLO G8. GUESS WHO! on the ceiling. Well, I guessed who," Cam said. "You! While we were swimming, you had plenty of time to raid our bunk."

"You think *I* did that!" Fran said. "You think I raided my own bunk!"

Cam nodded.

"But why?" Fran asked.

"Yes, why?" Terri asked Cam. "Why would Fran raid our bunk?"

"Because raids are fun," Fran said. "They're exciting. They're mysterious."

"They're messy," Terri said.

"Oh, Terri," Fran said, "you're so neat. I've seen you practicing math. All the numbers are lined up in columns just like the beds in our bunk." She smiled at the girls. "I wanted to have some fun. I wanted all of us to have some fun."

The other girls in G8 were sitting on the bench alongside the baseball field.

"What do we do now?" Terri asked.

"You don't have to do anything," Fran said. "While you're in arts and crafts, I'll clean up the bunk. Then I'll tell the other girls."

When G8 reached arts and crafts, Fran collected all their baseball gloves.

"I'll take these back to the bunk," she said. "And when arts and crafts is done, I have a surprise for all of you."

Betsy said, "I hope the surprise is ice cream."

When everyone was seated in the art room, Ruth, the arts and crafts counselor, gave each of the girls a wood base and wet reeds. She showed them how to weave the reeds and make a basket.

Cam and the others worked the entire period on their baskets. Ruth helped them. After about an hour, Fran returned.

"What's the surprise?" Betsy asked her.

"The bunk is all cleaned up," Fran answered. "All the beds are back where they belong."

"That's the surprise?" Betsy asked. She was disappointed.

"Did you catch the group that raided our bunk?" Gina asked.

"It wasn't a group," Fran said. "It was just one person. And I didn't catch her. Cam and Terri did."

"And Eric helped," Cam said.

Fran nodded. "It was me," she said. "They caught me. I thought a raid would be fun. I thought it would be exciting. I even thought it might help our team spirit when we played baseball and basketball against the other groups. But do you know what? It was just a

lot of mess and a lot of work to clean up. I'm sorry I did it."

"That's okay," Terri said. "The raid wasn't much fun, but watching Cam solve another mystery was."

"*Click!*" Gina said. "Now *I'm* solving a mystery."

"*Click! Click! Click! Click! Click!*" Gina said.

Gina took a deep breath and said, "That's all. I'm out of film."

"And it's time to get ready for dinner," Fran said.

Cam and the other girls in G8 followed Fran to their tidy bunk. They washed their hands and got ready for dinner.

"Just wait till after dinner," Fran said. "Our night activity will be so exciting."

"Are we going on a raid?" Betsy asked.

"No," Fran answered. "One raid is enough. We're going on a scavenger hunt."

After dinner, Sadie Rosen came to G8's bunk. She gave the girls in G8 this list of things to find:

1. A pair of mittens
2. A picture of Babe Ruth
3. A broken Tennis racket
4. A green shoelace
5. An air bag
6. A pen that writes green
7. A tulip
8. A radish
9. An old camera

"I have a balloon," Terri said. "That's an air bag."

Gina took a pen and pad from her night stand. She drew a circle on the paper and said, "This pen writes green."

"But that's blue ink," Fran said.

"Wait," Gina told her. "Watch it write green."

With her blue pen, Gina wrote the word *green.*

Cam, Terri, and the other girls in G8 laughed.

"And I'm an old camera," Cam said. "I'm ten years old and I have a photographic memory. That's just like a camera."

"Aren't scavenger hunts fun?" Fran asked.

"Camp is fun," Cam said. "It's lots of fun!"

CamJansen

The Basketball Mystery

CHAPTER ONE

"Hey! Quiet down!" Danny shouted. He was standing on a chair in the dining room. "I can't hear myself think!"

"That's good," Betsy shouted to him from her seat at the next table. "It's better if you don't think. I've heard enough of your riddles."

"Hey, you didn't hear this one. What did one baby ear of corn say to the other?"

Betsy didn't answer.

"It said, 'Where's pop corn?'"

"Sit down," Jacob told him.

Cam, the other girls in G8, and all the

other children at Camp Eagle Lake were in the dining room. They were waiting for their dinners. It was near the end of Cam's third week in camp. Soon she would be going home.

"What's for dinner?" Betsy asked.

"I know what's for dinner tomorrow night," Terri said. "The last night in camp is banquet night. We get hot dogs or steak or chicken or hamburger or turkey. We get whatever we want. It's like a restaurant."

Fran and Gina came out of the kitchen. They each held a large round tray.

"What's for dinner?" Betsy asked again.

"Food," Fran answered. "Good food."

Fran and Gina rested their trays on the edge of the table.

Fran said, "We have tuna fish or chicken, spinach or carrots, and baked potatoes."

"I'll take the chicken," Betsy said. "No one likes tuna fish."

"I do," Cam said. "Kitty does."

Fran took off the platters of chicken and tuna fish and bowls of spinach, carrots, and

baked potatoes. One by one, she gave them to the girls in her group.

Cam and her friends talked while they ate. When dinner was done, Cam put a little leftover tuna fish in a napkin. She put the napkin in her pocket.

When she got back to her bunk, Cam looked for Kitty. But Kitty wasn't in her usual place on the porch.

Cam put the tuna-fish-filled napkin on her night stand. Then she sat on her bed and thought about all the fun she had had in camp. She was sorry the three weeks were almost over.

"The basketball courts have lights," Terri said to Cam. "Let's shoot some hoops. This may be our last chance. Tomorrow night is the banquet."

"Sure," Cam said. "But first, I want to feed Kitty."

She took the tuna fish. Then Cam and Terri told Fran where they were going.

"Here, Kitty, Kitty, Kitty," Cam called once they were outside the bunk. Cam opened up the napkin and held it out.

"I wonder where she is," Cam said.

"Maybe she's not hungry. Or maybe someone else is feeding her," Terri said. "Let's just play basketball."

Cam closed the napkin and went with Terri to the basketball courts. There, under the lights, was Kitty. Eric and Jim, the sports counselor, were there, too. It was Eric's turn to help Jim. Both Jim and Eric had brooms. They were about to sweep the courts. Jim and a helper swept the courts every evening after dinner.

Eric was petting Kitty.

Jim said, "Sometimes Kitty comes here at

night. I think it's the light that attracts her."

Cam gave Kitty the tuna fish.

"I'm going home soon," Cam told Kitty. "I'll miss you."

Meow!

Kitty quickly ate the tuna fish. Then Cam told Jim that she and Terri wanted to play basketball.

"I want to play, too," Eric said.

"Here," Jim said, and gave Eric a key. "Get a basketball from the sports shed."

The others watched Eric walk slowly across the road to the shed. He stopped there for a moment and ran back.

"Everything is gone!" Eric told Jim. "When I got there, the door was open and all the sports equipment was gone."

CHAPTER TWO

"That can't be true," Jim said. "I locked the shed just before dinner, and everything was there."

They all hurried to the shed. The door was open. The padlock had been cut. It was on the floor. Inside, Jim's papers and empty boxes were everywhere. There was broken glass from the framed picture that had been on Jim's desk. And all the sports equipment was gone.

"Sadie Rosen will be upset," Jim said. "The equipment was new. There were prizes, too, for the banquet, and my computer."

"Don't worry," Terri said, "Cam will find

out who stole all your stuff. She's good at solving mysteries."

Eric corrected her. "Cam and *I* will find out," he said. "We solve mysteries together."

Jim collected his papers. Cam, Eric, and Terri looked for clues.

"Maybe the thief dropped something," Eric told Terri. "Maybe he stepped in mud and left footprints."

Jim picked up a sheet of paper and said, "Look at this. It's a list of all the equipment. There were twelve new basketballs, four dozen softballs, one dozen new bats, and lots more. My computer was new, too, and all the prizes for the banquet were taken."

"The thief must have loaded it all in his car and taken it out of camp," Terri said. "If he did, he drove right past Barry. We just have to ask Barry who left camp during dinner."

"Great!" Cam said. "Let's go."

"Please," Jim said. "Wait just a moment for me."

Jim put the papers he collected into an

empty box. Then he said, "Come on, Kitty. Come with us. There's broken glass on the floor. You can't stay here."

Kitty was by the door. She was licking the padlock.

"Come on, Kitty," Jim said again. Then he picked her up and carried her.

Barry was sitting in the booth by the camp entrance. He was reading a book. Jim knocked on the window.

"Hey, Jim," Barry said. He showed Jim his book. "You should read this. It's great. It's all about Babe Ruth. He was a baseball player."

Jim said, "I know who Babe Ruth was. What I want to know is who left camp during dinner."

"Dinner," Barry said and looked at his clipboard. "One car left during dinner and one truck came in. Sadie Rosen left at five fifty. She went to get the movie she's showing tonight." Barry leaned forward and whispered, "And the plumber came. There's a problem with the toilets in bunk B6."

"Did the plumber drive a truck?" Terri asked.

"Of course she drove a truck," Barry answered. "She has lots of tools and pipes and plungers. She needs all those things for her work. She's still here."

"Let's go to B6," Jim said. "Maybe the plumber has lots of basketballs and baseball bats, too."

"Basketballs? Baseball bats?" Barry said. "Why would a plumber need those?"

Jim and the others didn't answer. They were already on their way to B6.

CHAPTER THREE

"Look!" Terri said, and pointed. "There's the plumber's truck. It's big enough to hold lots of sports stuff."

A small truck was parked in front of bunk B6. Cam, Eric, Terri, and Jim hurried across the baseball field. Jim put Kitty down. Then he tried to open the back door of the truck. It was locked.

"Are you looking for me?" someone asked.

Cam and the others turned. A tall woman was standing behind them. She wore overalls, a T-shirt, work boots and a baseball cap.

She was holding a large metal toolbox.

"We're looking for basketballs and base-ball bats," Cam said.

"I don't have any of those," the woman said as she walked past Cam and the others. She opened the back door of her truck and put her things inside.

Jim held the door open.

"May I look inside?" he asked.

"Sure," the woman said. "Lots of people are curious about plumbing. But it's just about keeping the water running, stopping leaks, and sometimes installing boilers for heat. That's what I do."

There were lots of pipes and tools in the truck, but no sports equipment.

"Do you know what I just did in there?" the woman asked, and pointed to bunk B6. "I just cleared a clogged toilet. Do you know what it was clogged with? Carrot sticks! I didn't ask why there were carrots in the toilet. I never ask. I just clear the clog and go home."

"Thank you," Jim said, and closed the back door of the truck.

"Once I found a math test. A boy had balled it up. He dropped it in the bowl and flushed. It was all wet when I got it out. But do you know what? His mother opened it up to see his grade on the test."

"Thank you," Jim said again.

"His mother wasn't angry that he stopped up the toilet," the plumber said. "But she was real angry about the test grade. Oh, I could tell you lots of stories."

"We're looking for basketballs," Eric said.

"Oh, I never found one of those in a toilet. It wouldn't fit through the pipes."

The plumber petted Kitty.

"One day, I'm going to write a book," she said. "I might call it *Peeks at Leaks* or *Pipes and Gripes*."

She got in her truck. "Look for my book," she said as she drove off.

Jim said, "The only other person who came in or left during dinner was Sadie Rosen. She wouldn't steal basketballs and my computer."

"Is there a back way into camp?" Cam asked.

"You can go through the woods," Jim told her.

They followed Jim to the woods just beyond the baseball field. It had rained earlier in the day. The ground was soft and wet.

Jim said, "Look for foot or tire prints."

They all walked along the edge of the woods from the end near the baseball field to the road.

Once they reached the road, Eric said, "There's nothing here. There's no path wide enough for a car or truck to ride on."

"There are lots of footprints," Terri said. "They're from this afternoon, when we played baseball here. But none of them leads into the woods."

There were several benches along the side of the road. Jim sat on one. He put his head in his hands and said, "We didn't find any clues. Everything is just gone."

Meow!

Kitty rubbed her back against Jim's leg.

"No, it's not just gone," Cam told him. "We did learn something. We learned that the sports equipment didn't leave the camp through the front entrance or through the woods. So it must still be here. It must be hidden."

Jim looked up.

"That's right," Jim said. "Now where in camp could someone hide basketballs, softballs, baseball bats, my computer, and all those prizes?"

CHAPTER FOUR

"This is like a math problem," Terri said. "First we have to see what we know and then find out what we don't know."

"We know lots of stuff was stolen," Eric said.

"And we know it's still somewhere in camp," Terri added. "We just need to know where."

"This isn't helping," Jim said. "I don't need problems. I need answers. I need to know where to find my things."

Meow! Kitty said, and licked Cam's hand.

Cam petted Kitty.

Jim said, "I also need to know what to do without all the sports equipment. The end-of-camp tournaments are tomorrow."

Meow!

Cam took her hand from Kitty. Her palm was wet. Cam wiped her hand on her shirt.

"She's licking your hand," Eric said. "It must taste like the tuna fish you fed her."

"That's right," Cam said, and looked at Kitty.

Cam looked at her hand. She thought for a moment and said, "Eric, you may have done it again. You may have helped me remember a very important clue."

"What clue?" Terri asked.

Cam didn't answer. Instead she closed her eyes and said, *"Click!"*

She said, *"Click!"* again.

"What are you looking at?" Eric asked.

"I'm looking at Kitty by the sports shed," Cam answered.

Cam opened her eyes. "I just remembered that when we left the shed, Kitty didn't want to go. Jim had to pick her up and carry her."

"So what?" Jim asked. "She's not heavy."

"But why didn't she want to leave?" Cam asked as she stood. "I'm going back to the shed to find out."

Jim picked up Kitty again. He followed Cam, Eric, and Terri to the shed.

"Please," Cam said, "put Kitty down."

Jim put Kitty down by the entrance to the shed. Kitty went back to the padlock. She started to lick it.

"When we went to talk to Barry, Kitty was licking this lock," Cam said. "That's why Kitty didn't want to leave the shed."

"But why?" Eric asked. "It's just a metal lock."

Jim took the padlock from Kitty. He smelled it.

"It's metal," he said, "but it smells like fish."

"Tuna fish," Terri said. "Cam, you had tuna fish in a napkin. You must have touched it."

"But I didn't," Cam said. "None of us did. We just looked at the lock and saw it was cut. The last person to touch it must have been the thief."

"And there must have been tuna fish on his hands," Eric said, "or the smell of tuna fish."

Terri said, "We know the thief is still in camp. All we have to do is figure out who in camp has the smell of tuna fish on his hands."

"Well," Eric said. "It can't be one of the campers. We were all eating dinner when the thief broke into the shed. And a camper wouldn't have a place to hide that sports stuff."

"And the counselors were all with their groups," Terri added.

"Maybe Barry did it," Eric said, "He wasn't in the dining room."

"Barry has been at Eagle Lake for a very long time," Jim said. "I think he's Sadie Rosen's uncle or cousin. He wouldn't steal from the camp."

"But that's everyone," Terri said.

Meow!

Jim looked at Kitty. Then he said, "No, it isn't. There's still the kitchen staff. They prepared the chicken and tuna fish. But when dinner was being served, one of them could have snuck off and cut the lock. And if the thief prepared the tuna, his hands would have a fishy smell."

Jim rubbed his chin. "If I'm right, and the thief works in the kitchen, I think I know just where the sports equipment is hidden."

"Where?" Eric asked. "Where could someone hide all those basketballs and base-ball bats?"

"I'll show you," Jim said. "Follow me."

CHAPTER FIVE

Jim walked across the baseball field, through the dining room, and into the kitchen. Cam, Eric, Terri, and Kitty followed him. Jim stopped in front of a large metal door. He pulled on the door handle, but it didn't open.

"It's locked," Jim said.

"But it's a refrigerator," Terri said. "Why would anyone keep basketballs in a refrigerator?"

"It's a big walk-in refrigerator," Jim said. "The butcher comes to camp every morning and delivers meat and fish. It's put in here. In the afternoon, the cook makes dinner. Then the refrigerator is empty. The thief could have sneaked out during dinner, stolen the sports equipment, the prizes, and my computer and hidden it all in here. Later tonight, when everyone is asleep, he can load it in his car and drive away."

"Should we hide here and wait for the thief to unlock it?" Eric asked.

"No," Jim answered. "I'll get Sadie Rosen. She has a key to the refrigerator. When she opens it, we'll find out if I'm right."

Jim took a cell phone from his pocket. He was about to make a call when the kitchen door opened. Kenny, one of the kitchen workers, came in. He was holding a key.

"Oops!" he said.

Kenny started to turn. He was about to leave the kitchen.

"Wait!" Jim said. "Why did you come in here?"

"I thought I was hungry, but I'm not," Kenny answered.

"Is that the key to the refrigerator?" Jim asked.

"Is it? I don't know," Kenny said.

Jim took the key from him. He put it in the lock just beneath the refrigerator door handle. He turned the key and opened the door.

"Basketballs," Jim said. "Baseball bats, softballs, tennis balls, hockey pucks, prizes, and my computer. They're all nice and cold."

"Why is that stuff in the refrigerator?" Kenny asked.

"That's a good question," Jim said. "And

I think you already know the answer."

Kenny turned and quickly left the kitchen.

"We have to stop him," Eric said.

"No, we don't," Jim said. "Barry will."

Jim pressed a few buttons on his cell phone. Then he spoke into it.

"Barry, this is Jim. Please close the gate. Kenny is going to try to leave camp, and you have to stop him."

Then Jim called Sadie Rosen and told her about the stolen sports equipment. He also told her how Cam, Eric, Terri, and Kitty helped him catch the thief.

"Sadie Rosen told me to thank you," Jim said once he had finished talking with her. "She said she'll take care of everything. She has an extra lock for my sports shed. She will bring it here. Then I can put everything back."

"We'll help," Cam said.

"No, thank you," Jim said. "Go back to your bunks. There's a movie tonight. I don't want you to miss it."

Cam, Eric, and Terri walked toward the door to the dining room.

"Kitty," Cam said. "Here, Kitty."

Kitty ran to Cam. She followed her and Terri back to their bunk.

CHAPTER SIX

The next night, Cam wore her nicest shirt and pants to the banquet. At the table, on each plate, was a menu with lots of choices. Fran stood by Cam's seat. She was wearing a white shirt and holding a pad and pencil. She was G8's waitress for the banquet.

"And what would you like for dinner?" Fran asked.

"I'll have a hamburger on a toasted bun," Cam said, "with lots of onions and tomatoes."

"Thank you."

Fran wrote what Cam wanted for dinner on her pad.

"This is fun," Terri said.

Terri ordered chicken and rice.

When Fran had taken orders from all the girls in her group, she stood by her own chair.

"And what would you like?" Fran asked her empty chair.

Fran quickly sat down, looked up, and answered, "Steak, rice, and salad."

Fran jumped up. She wrote her own order on her pad and went to the kitchen.

The girls giggled.

"She's funny," Betsy said.

After dinner, Sadie Rosen stood in the center of the dining room. Jim and Ruth, the arts and crafts counselor, brought in some boxes and put them on the tables beside Sadie Rosen.

Ms. Rosen spoke into a microphone.

"This is the last night of camp," she said. "We're all sorry your three-week visit here must end. But when you get home, I want you to think about Camp Eagle Lake. I hope you'll remember the good time you had here."

Sadie Rosen held up a pack a photographs.

"To help you remember," she said, "each of you will get a photograph of your group."

"Those are the pictures of us that were taken the first day of camp," Terri whispered.

"What about the awards?" Jacob shouted.

"Yes!" Matthew called out. "Let's get the awards."

Sadie Rosen smiled.

Jim and Ruth distributed the boxes. The awards for G8 and B8 were boxed together. G8's table was next to B8's.

Fran stood between the two tables. She opened the box and took out the first award, a jar of chocolate syrup and a certificate.

"This is for Betsy," she announced. "It's the Sundae on Monday Award. Betsy loves ice cream. With this chocolate syrup she can have ice-cream sundaes every day of the week, even on Mondays."

Jacob reached in and took out a book and another certificate.

"This is the Camp Eagle Lake Comedy Award and this is *The Camp Eagle Lake Joke Book*."

Jacob gave Danny the certificate. Fran gave him the book.

"Please promise us," Fran said, "that until you go home, you will only tell jokes found in this book."

"Sure. I promise."

Then Danny opened the book.

"Hey," Danny said. "This book is empty. All the pages are blank."

Jacob and Fran laughed.

"Yes, that's *our* joke," Jacob said.

Terri was given the Number Whiz Award. It was a wood frame with columns of beads all across it.

"It's an abacus," Fran said.

"I know," Terri told her. "Before there were calculators, lots of people used these to do math."

Sadie Rosen came to G8's table carrying a large envelope. "I wanted to present this award," she said. "It's Camp Eagle Lake's

first Best Detective Award and it's for Cam Jansen."

She gave Cam a certificate and a notepad with a black leather cover. "This is a real police officer's pad," she said. "When you're solving a mystery, you can write the clues in it."

"And this," Sadie Rosen said, "is for Eric." She took a silver deputy badge from the envelope and gave it to Eric. "It's Camp Eagle Lake's Best Deputy Award."

Eric pinned the badge to his shirt.

"Thank you," Cam said, and smiled. "And thank you for three wonderful weeks."

"Yes, thank you," Eric said.

The next morning, Cam wrote all her friends' e-mail addresses and telephone numbers in her police officer's pad. She promised to write or call them often.

"I hope we'll come back next summer," Eric said to Cam before they got into Mr. Jansen's car.

"I hope so, too," Cam said.

Cam's father and Eric's father helped

their children load their suitcases and other things into the trunk of Mr. Jansen's car.

Cam stood by the car. She took one last look at Camp Eagle Lake. She took a deep breath, then she blinked her eyes and said *"Click!"*

Cam pointed to her head and smiled. "Now I'll have a picture of camp right here forever."

A Cam Jansen Memory Game

Take another look at the picture opposite the main title page. Study it. Blink your eyes and say, *"Click!"* Then turn back to this page and answer these questions. Please, first study the picture, *then* look at the questions.

1. Is anyone in the picture wearing long pants?
2. Is there a tennis racket in the picture? A baseball glove?
3. In the Camp Eagle Lake sign, is the eagle facing to the right or to the left?
4. Is anyone in the picture wearing a hat?
5. How many people are in the picture?
6. Which letter in the Camp Eagle Lake sign is hidden?